# Santa's Christmas Cows

## HEIDI KOVACS

PAGE PUBLISHING
Conneaut Lake, PA

First originally published by Page Publishing 2022

ISBN 978-1-6624-7271-8 (pbk)
ISBN 979-8-88793-416-7 (hc)
ISBN 978-1-6624-7272-5 (digital)

Printed in the United States of America

To my daughters Madeline and Miranda. You have been the greatest gift in the world to me and my biggest inspiration in life. Always remember, you are powerful, brave, and beautiful! Believe in yourselves and chase your dreams!

All my love,

—Mom

Did you know that not only is Santa a world-famous toy maker, but he's also a dairy farmer? It all started many years ago on a snowy winter night in the North Pole's forest. While searching for the perfect Christmas tree for Mrs. Claus to decorate the Candlelight Cottage with, Santa heard a startling noise under a mighty grove of pine trees. It sounded like one of his reindeer had bellowed, but this noise was a noise he couldn't quite figure out.

The grove was thick with trees, and the swirling snow made it difficult to see. Santa soon discovered the strange sound was coming from two stray Jersey cows that were seeking shelter from the snowstorm. Santa hadn't heard of any local dairy farms that were missing animals, so he thought it best to bring them back to his stable for food and shelter. He whistled and called to his sleigh for Jingle, the Border collie. "Jingle, girl, come!" She is his special dog that helps herd the reindeer when they're out on pasture, and she guides them back to the Starlight Stable every night. As soon as Santa whistled, Jingle sprang into action and started to herd the cows back to the stable.

The Starlight Stable was handcrafted by the elves. It was made of beautiful pine boards, it had a cedar shake roof, and the elves kept it freshly bedded with cedar shavings. Every window had a small holly wreath on it with a big red bow. In the corner of the stable stood a small lit spruce tree. It sparkled with little white lights, and it was decorated with candy canes, gold stars, and red Christmas ornaments. Each pen had its own wooden plaque on the door, and the individual reindeer's names were carefully engraved on each of them. Santa happened to have two empty stalls for his new beautiful cows. He put them in their stalls for the night and suddenly realized that he didn't know what he was going to feed them!

"What am I going to feed them?" he asked his elves. "The North Pole doesn't have grass in the winter months, and we've only stored enough hay for the reindeer!"

Prancer
Blitzen

Dancer
Blitzen

Just as he was beginning to worry, Mrs. Claus had come to see what all the commotion was, and as always, she had a very large plate of her best sugar cookies for everyone. They were in shapes of bells and stars and had sprinkles and colored sugar on top.

As Santa took a bite, he thought out loud, "Do you think maybe the Jerseys like to eat cookies?"

As he offered them each a cookie, they accepted them with great appreciation. Santa and Mrs. Claus chuckled together.

"Looks like I'll need to bake more sugar cookies to feed your cows," Mrs. Claus stated.

Just then, their cookie plans were interrupted by an announcement over the Icicle Intercom. "Paging Santa. Paging Santa. There's a problem in the Peppermint Shack! Report at once," the elves exclaimed! The candy temperature had gotten too high for the elves, and an entire batch of candy canes would have to be thrown out into the forest for the animals!

Santa said, "If my cows will eat Christmas cookies, then why not try candy canes as well?"

Vanila
Sugar

He grabbed two metal buckets, filled them up with candy canes from the Peppermint Shack, and brought them to the cows. They ate their sugar cookies and candy canes as fast as Santa could bring them to the cows. He was very pleased to have his own milk cows at the North Pole.

The next morning, Santa woke up extra early because he knew that his cows would need to be milked. He put on his big black boots and his soft red suit, then he headed out through the snow to the stable. The stable was calm, quiet, and warm with the only light being from the little tree twinkling in the corner. Santa snuck in quietly as to not wake the reindeer and found his Jerseys anxiously waiting to be milked. He pulled out his custom milk stool and began to milk them by hand. As he filled up his pail, he sang Christmas carols and whistled festive tunes. The cows really liked their farmer, and they loved the joy that Starlight Stable brought to their lives.

When the morning work was done, Santa went to the stable cabinet to add a little Christmas cheer to his new cows. He gave them each their own string of jingle bells around their necks and tied beautiful red bows on their tails. But they needed names if they were going to stay at the Starlight Stable. With Christmas rapidly approaching, he chose the names Noel and Nativity. They would be perfect names for his dairy cows. Once he and the elves had finished the barn chores, they headed to the house for breakfast.

Mrs. Claus made everyone her special ornament omelet. She used the fresh eggs that she collected every morning from the Holiday Henhouse. Tending to her chickens was her favorite task on their festive farm, and she even had a pet chicken named Mittens! When Mittens came to the North Pole, she always had cold feet. Mrs. Claus wanted to make her more comfortable, so she knit her, her own special pair of wool snowflake mittens to keep her feet warm. Mittens became so happy and broody with her knitted gift that the name stuck.

HOLIDAY HENHOUSE

Fresh eggs and fresh milk had everyone egg-cited, and they could hardly wait to start eating. Santa poured the first glass and took a huge gulp of the creamy surprise. He was puzzled.

"This milk is like nothing I've ever tasted before! It's so sweet and creamy!"

Each glass put a huge smile on everyone's faces. They even chuckled a little bit as it appeared to be a cup of pure joy.

Santa said, "These beautiful cows have brought us a milk so merry that it tickles me so," followed by a deep "Hohoho."

As the Peppermint Shack was busy cooking and grinding up candy canes, Mrs. Claus was just as busy baking countless cookies for Noel and Nativity. Faster than you could imagine, there was so much Merry Milk that they didn't know what to do with it all. Santa didn't want it to go to waste by having to throw it away.

"My dear," he said to Mrs. Claus. "Do you think we could share our Merry Milk with the world?"

She answered by saying, "That is certainly the only way to solve our overstock problem."

Santa agreed and said, "We should open our own creamery here at the North Pole. We can bottle it for the world!"

Vanila
Sugar
20

MISTLETOE MILK COMPANY
MILK
MILK
MILK
MILK

They named it the Mistletoe Milk Company, and bottling and distribution began at once. Extra Merry Milk was fed to the reindeer, and Mrs. Claus would feed it to her chickens in the Holiday Henhouse. There was so much excitement around town, and the milk was bringing so much joy to everyone. The reindeer were flying extra high, and Mrs. Claus said even her chicken, Mittens, was clucking Christmas songs.

"You wouldn't believe it, Santa," she said, "but ever since I started feeding Merry Milk to the chickens in the Holiday Henhouse, my birds have been laying double the number of eggs. And the eggs are huge!" Production in the Holiday Henhouse was through the roof! "It's like Merry Milk is a special egg-making nog or something," Mrs. Claus declared. It was at that moment that the Clauses decided to change the name of Merry Milk to Eggnog instead.

HOLIDAY HENHOUSE

It was such a delicious treat for families in the North Pole that Santa decided he would distribute his eggnog every Christmas morning as a holiday surprise. Families grew to love the yearly tradition of the Mistletoe Milk Company's eggnog every Christmas morning with their full stockings and presents under the tree. Eggnog is now distributed worldwide thanks to its Merry Milk origin with Santa's Christmas cows, Noel and Nativity.

# About the Author

Heidi Kovacs is the dreamer whose vision brought Sugar Maple Jerseys to life. She is the founder and co-owner of their 180-acre dairy farm in Stockton, New Jersey, where she farms with her husband, Rick, and their two daughters, Madeline and Miranda. It is her creative personality, her love for her children, and her passion for Jersey cows that brought her book, *Santa's Christmas Cows*, to fruition. All the animals and children on the farm are the product of Heidi's care and an example of her strength, courage, responsibility, hard work, and understanding. Sugar Maple Jerseys was established in 2013 and continues to be operational today. It is there on their small farm that they milk forty registered Jersey cows twice a day and run their on-site country store. You can visit www.sugarmaplejerseys.com for more information.

www.ingramcontent.com/pod-product-compliance
Lightning Source LLC
Chambersburg PA
CBHW040904070726
47599CB00038B/2296